Is Mr. Marshall in trouble?

"I wish Mrs. Becker would come back," Lois said to everyone in the park.

They all nodded, even though nobody ever wanted to agree with crybaby Lois.

Suddenly, Winston gasped. "Hey! Look!"

They all looked in the direction he was pointing. Elizabeth saw their substitute teacher, Mr. Marshall, walking along the sidewalk. "I wonder what he's doing here," she said.

But the next moment, they all had something else to wonder about.

A police car was slowing down behind him. It stopped, and the window rolled down. Mr. Marshall leaned over to talk to the officers inside.

Why did the police want to talk to their substitute teacher?

SWEET VALLEY KIDS

THE TWINS' MYSTERY TEACHER

Written by
Molly Mia Stewart

Created by
FRANCINE PASCAL

Illustrated by
Ying-Hwa Hu

A BANTAM SKYLARK BOOK
NEW YORK · TORONTO · LONDON · SYDNEY · AUCKLAND

RL 2, 005-008

THE TWINS' MYSTERY TEACHER
A Bantam Skylark Book / January 1990

*Sweet Valley High® and Sweet Valley Kids™ are trademarks of
Francine Pascal*

Conceived by Francine Pascal

*Produced by Daniel Weiss Associates, Inc.,
33 West 17th Street,
New York, NY 10011*

Cover art by Susan Tang

*Skylark Books is a registered trademark of Bantam Books, a division of
Bantam Doubleday Dell Publishing Group, Inc.*

ISBN 0-553-15760-4

Published simultaneously in the United States and Canada

---

*Bantam Books are published by Bantam Books, a division of Bantam Double-
day Dell Publishing Group, Inc. Its trademark, consisting of the words
"Bantam Books" and the portrayal of a rooster, is Registered in U.S. Patent
and Trademark Office and in other countries. Marca Registrada. Bantam
Books, 666 Fifth Avenue, New York, New York 10103.*

PRINTED IN THE UNITED STATES OF AMERICA

OPM   0 9 8 7 6 5 4 3 2 1

To John Stewart Carmen

CHAPTER 1

Emergency in the Classroom

Elizabeth Wakefield was working on a subtraction problem at the blackboard. Suddenly, her chalk went *screeeeech*! A shiver went up and down her back.

Elizabeth looked over at her second-grade teacher. Mrs. Becker was rubbing her forehead and sniffling. She wasn't watching the board.

"What answer did you get for this one?" Jessica Wakefield whispered to Elizabeth. Jessica was Elizabeth's twin sister, and she was doing a subtraction problem on the board, too. So were Caroline Pearce, Ken Matthews, and Andy Franklin.

"Can't you do the problem?" Elizabeth asked Jessica softly.

Jessica pouted. "I just need a teeny tiny hint, Lizzie."

Jessica was always asking Elizabeth for hints. Lots of people thought twins were exactly alike, but on the inside, Elizabeth and Jessica were very different. Elizabeth paid attention in class and she always did her homework. She could be by herself for a long time without getting lonely. Jessica was just the opposite. She daydreamed in class and often got caught passing notes to her friends. So Jessica often needed help from Elizabeth, especially in math.

Elizabeth didn't really mind helping her

sister, though. Being twins meant they were best friends. They were the only identical twins in Sweet Valley Elementary School. They both had long blond hair with bangs, and deep blue-green eyes. They had many matching outfits, but Jessica picked hers in pink, and Elizabeth usually chose blue. Still, most people couldn't tell them apart. Only if you looked at their name bracelets could you be sure who was who.

Being twins was special. Sometimes Elizabeth knew what Jessica was going to say before Jessica said it. Sometimes Jessica could tell what Elizabeth was thinking, too.

"Twenty-four minus thirteen is eleven," Elizabeth told her sister. "Remember?"

Jessica smiled. "Yes! Now I remember."

"Hey, no fair!" Caroline complained. Caroline stood on Jessica's other side.

Jessica turned and stuck her tongue out at Caroline. "Mind your own beeswax."

"I'll help you, too, if you want," Elizabeth told Caroline.

Caroline just lifted her chin without saying a word.

Elizabeth looked at Jessica, and Jessica looked at Elizabeth. They were both thinking that Caroline was such a busybody!

"OK, everyone, time to check your answers," Mrs. Becker said. She stood up and started walking to the blackboard. "Is everyone fin—"

She stopped talking in the middle of her sentence and stared straight ahead. Elizabeth looked at her in surprise.

Mrs. Becker had been sniffling and sneezing and coughing ever since the winter vacation. But now she looked worse than ever. Her face looked very, *very* pale.

"Oh, dear. I can't—" Mrs. Becker took a step forward, and then a step backward.

Elizabeth's eyes widened. "Mrs. Becker? Are you OK?"

"What's wrong with her?" Jessica whispered. She sounded frightened.

Just then, Mrs. Becker began to reach for the side of her desk.

"She's fainting!" Elizabeth shouted.

Sure enough, Mrs. Becker collapsed onto the floor.

"Is she dead?" Charlie Cashman yelled, as some girls screamed.

Everyone jumped out of their chairs and rushed over to Mrs. Becker.

"Give her mouth-to-mouth breathing!" Lila Fowler said in a bossy voice.

"I know!" Ken Matthews shouted. "Let's get some salt from the cafeteria! Salt is good for people who faint!"

"That's *smelling* salts," Andy Franklin said.

Lois Waller was crying and hiccuping at the same time.

Elizabeth knelt down next to their teacher. Mrs. Becker looked very pale, but she was still breathing. "Mrs. Becker? Are you awake?"

"What are we going to do?" Lois whimpered.

"Don't cry!" Jessica told her. "That won't make Mrs. Becker better!"

Elizabeth looked up at her classmates. "I know," she exclaimed. "I'll go get the principal!"

Elizabeth jumped up and ran out the door.

CHAPTER 2

Jessica to the Rescue

Jessica jumped up, too. "What should we do?" she asked Lila, who was her next-best friend after Elizabeth.

"Let's see if she does have smelling salts," Lila whispered. She pushed Jessica toward Mrs. Becker's desk.

Jessica's eyes grew wide. Mrs. Becker's desk was strictly off-limits. The middle drawer even had a sign on it that said "No Trespassing!"

But Mrs. Becker would know they were trying to help her. Jessica opened the middle drawer while Lila looked over her shoulder.

Inside were Mrs. Becker's private belongings: her purse, her gradebook, a little bottle of hand lotion, a nail clipper, and a few other things.

"Look—what's that?" Lila hissed. She pointed to a tiny glass bottle filled with yellow liquid.

Jessica grabbed it. "It's perfume," she said excitedly. "Do you think it would help?"

"What are you doing?" Caroline said. "You're going through the No Trespassing drawer! You're not supposed to!"

"This is an emergency," Lila answered. "We have to wake up Mrs. Becker!"

Jessica opened the little bottle and sniffed it. "Whew!" she gasped. "This smells strong!" The perfume made her eyes water.

Some of the boys started making faces because the whole room was beginning to smell perfumy.

"Hey!" Winston Egbert announced. "Mrs. Becker said something!"

Jessica knelt down next to Winston and held the bottle under Mrs. Becker's nose. The teacher's face was getting some of its normal color back.

"Don't forget the cheese," Mrs. Becker mumbled.

Winston's eyes popped open. So did his mouth. "*Cheese?* Did you hear that? It sounds like an alien took over her body!"

"You watch too many scary movies," Jessica giggled. She waved the bottle again. "Mrs. Becker! Wake up!"

"Winston could be right," Charlie said, nodding. "A lot of aliens invade sleeping bodies. Then when you wake up you aren't the same person anymore."

Amy Sutton made a face. "That's dumb! Boys are *so* dumb!"

11

"Boys are not dumb!" Todd Wilkins said angrily. "Girls don't know anything."

Jessica stood up. "You be quiet, Todd!"

All the girls started yelling at the boys, and all the boys yelled back. Before anyone noticed, Mrs. Becker was sitting up.

"What's going on?" she asked, a bit surprised.

Everyone stopped talking. Jessica rubbed her perfumy hand on her pants. "You fainted," she told the teacher. Then she smiled proudly. "But I woke you up with this!" She held out the little bottle.

Mrs. Becker nodded slowly and rubbed her forehead. "Thank you, Jessica. I think I should—"

"Elizabeth went to get Mrs. Armstrong," Todd said. Mrs. Armstrong was the principal.

12

"Here they come!" Jim Sturbridge yelled from his look-out post by the door.

In a moment, Mrs. Armstrong and the school nurse, Miss Diener, hurried in. Elizabeth came in after them.

"Is she OK?" Elizabeth asked Jessica in a whisper.

Jessica nodded. "I woke her up with this perfume," she said, holding up the bottle. "Wasn't that smart?"

"It sure was," Elizabeth agreed with a smile.

While Miss Diener helped Mrs. Becker up, Mrs. Armstrong clapped her hands together for attention.

"OK, class! Back to your seats, please!" she said. "We had a bit of a scare, but Mrs. Becker will be fine. She just needs to get some air."

Caroline raised her hand. "Oh! Oh!" she gasped.

"Yes?" Mrs. Armstrong called on Caroline.

"Can I be class monitor?" Caroline asked.

Jessica made a face at Caroline's back. Caroline was such a teacher's pet. Now she wanted to be principal's pet, too!

"Well, let's see." Mrs. Armstrong looked at the clock. "We only have half an hour left until the end of the day, so I think I'll just stay here. You can all do your homework until the bell rings."

"Ohhhh!" Everybody groaned. Homework sounded boring after the excitement about Mrs. Becker.

"I wonder if Mrs. Becker is really sick," Jessica whispered to Elizabeth.

Elizabeth shook her head slowly. She

looked worried. "I hope not. I don't want her to be sick."

"Me, neither," Jessica agreed. "But if she is, we'll get a substitute teacher."

Ken overheard her. "Right!" he whispered. "A substitute! Get your paper airplanes ready."

Soon everyone in the class was wondering who would be teaching them the next day. Jessica was excited. Some substitutes were boring, and some were interesting. You never knew what a substitute would be like. But that was part of the fun.

"I can't wait till tomorrow," she said with a grin.

CHAPTER 3

Wild Second Graders

As soon as Elizabeth and Jessica got off the bus the next morning, they ran into the school.

"Pssst!" Ellen Riteman hissed from the classroom doorway. "Come here, you two!"

Elizabeth and Jessica hurried over. Their classmates were also crowded outside the door. Charlie was looking through the crack between the door and the doorframe.

"What is it?" Jessica whispered. "Do we have a substitute?"

"Yes!" Lila said mischievously. "We have a plan."

Elizabeth smiled. "What is it?" she asked.

"Listen, you guys," Charlie said in a loud whisper. "Everybody sit in different seats."

All the kids nodded with big grins on their faces.

"Do we have to?" Lois asked timidly.

Charlie gave her a mean look. "Yes," he growled. "Everyone."

"I'm sitting in my own seat," Caroline said. "And I'm telling the substitute what you are doing!"

Jerry McAllister punched Caroline in the arm. "I'll get you at recess if you do."

"Come on," Ellen said. "It's just for fun."

"Yeah!" everyone chimed in.

Elizabeth peeked through the door. The substitute teacher was a very thin man with curly red hair that stuck out at the sides. He kept rearranging the papers on Mrs.

18

Becker's desk and glancing up at the wall clock. He looked very nervous.

"Isn't he funny-looking?" Jessica whispered.

"I guess," Elizabeth agreed. She usually didn't like to play jokes on people, but it would last just a little while. She guessed there would be no harm.

One by one, the kids walked into the classroom. Charlie and Jerry were grinning very big grins. Jerry sat in Lila's regular seat. Charlie took Andy Franklin's place in the front row.

Andy was the only one who didn't know about the plan because he arrived late. When he saw everybody in different seats, he looked confused. Then he saw Charlie sitting in his seat. Charlie gave him a "don't tell" look. Without a word, Andy hugged his books and went to find an empty seat.

Elizabeth sat in the last row. The whole class looked different from the back. It was kind of fun! She looked over at Amy Sutton and giggled.

"Good morning, children," the substitute said as he stood in front of the class. His voice was shaky. "Mrs. Becker has the flu, so I'm taking her place. My name is Mr. Pinecone."

Some of the boys and girls giggled. Mr. Pinecone looked embarrassed about his name.

"I'm going to take attendance," Mr. Pinecone went on quickly.

He turned to write something on the blackboard. Three big wads of paper flew immediately across the room from different directions. One of them hit the blackboard, and Mr. Pinecone turned around quickly.

"What was that?" he asked nervously.

Caroline raised her hand. "Those boys threw them," she said, pointing at Winston, Todd, and Ken.

"She's such a tattletale," Amy whispered to Elizabeth. Elizabeth nodded. She was beginning to feel sorry for Mr. Pinecone. She was also beginning to wish they weren't sitting in the wrong seats.

Mr. Pinecone picked up the seating chart and looked at Charlie. "Andrew Franklin?" he asked.

All of the boys began to laugh. Charlie pretended to look confused. "No, I'm Charlie. The chart must be wrong."

There was more laughter. Elizabeth's face was beginning to feel warm. She slumped down in her seat. Across the room, Jessica, Lila, and Ellen were talking without even

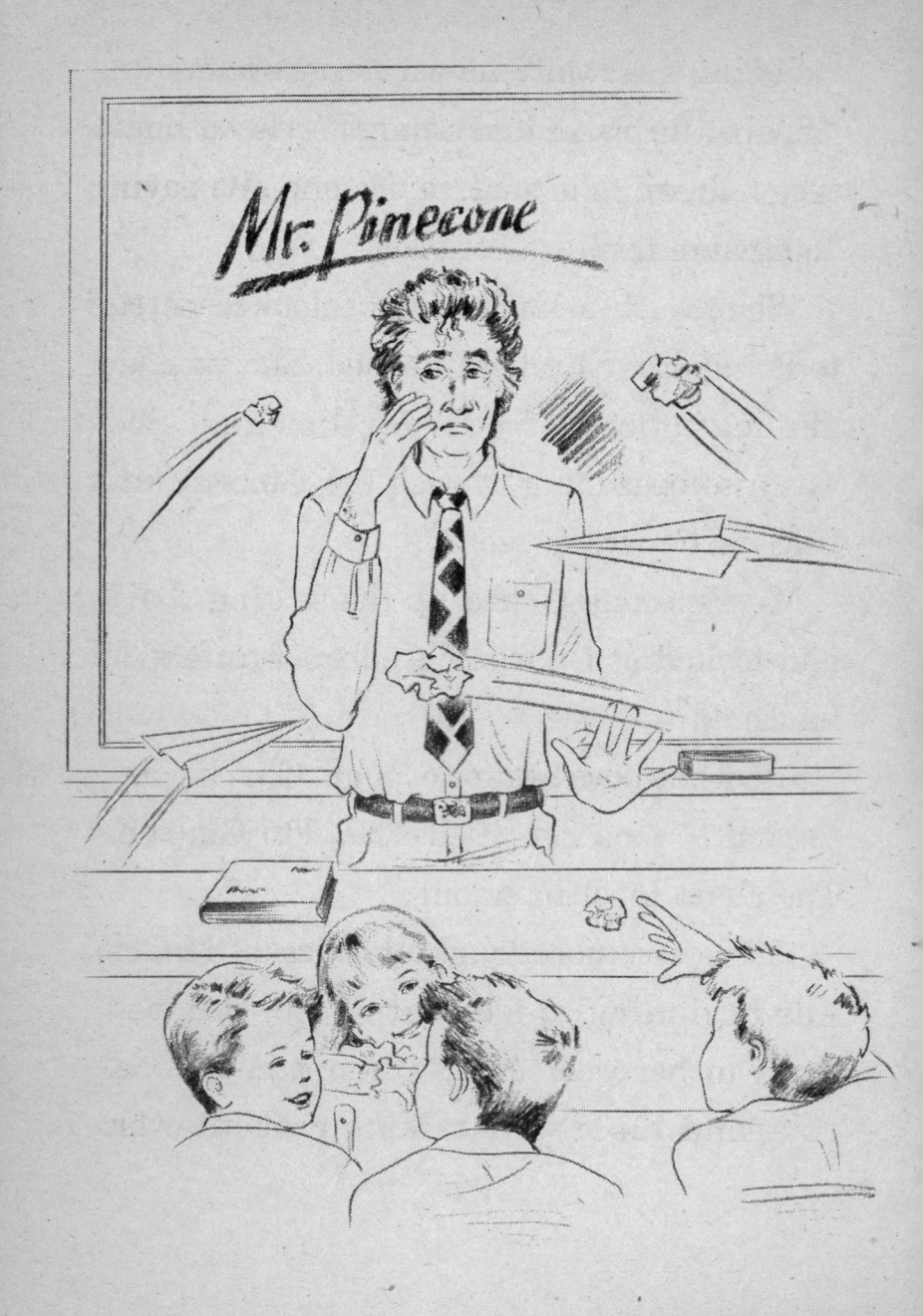

keeping their voices down. Jerry was making a paper airplane, and Sandy Ferris was making a drawing of a horse. No one was paying attention to the substitute.

"Umm . . ." Mr. Pinecone looked at the seating chart, and then at Lila. "Are you Todd Wilkins?"

Lila shook her head. "Do I look like a boy?"

Jessica and Ellen both giggled.

"Mr. Pinecone?" Ken Matthews called out as he waved his hand in the air. "I have to go to the bathroom."

"Oh." Mr. Pinecone looked worried. "OK."

"So do I!" Todd said.

Winston Egbert raised his hand. "Me, too! Right away!"

"Only one person at a time can go," Caroline said loudly. Todd made a monster face at her, and Jerry's paper airplane flew into the back of her head.

Elizabeth wished they could start the day over. Their joke wasn't funny anymore. It was just mean.

One of the boys made an explosion sound. Lois started to cry.

"What's wrong?" Mr. Pinecone asked her. He looked at the seating chart and then at Lois. "Elizabeth?"

"Here!" Elizabeth said, raising her hand, trying to be helpful.

"I'm Elizabeth!" Jessica said, raising her hand. She turned in her seat and pointed at Elizabeth. "That's Jessica."

"No, *I'm* Elizabeth," Elizabeth said firmly. She stared hard at her twin.

"Come on, Jess," Jessica said. "I don't think you're being funny."

Mr. Pinecone sat down and sighed. "Wait a minute. What's going on?"

Ellen, Lila, and Jessica all started giggling again. Elizabeth shook her head. It was going to be a silly day!

CHAPTER 4

No More Mr. Nice Guy

"Is Mr. Pinecone here?" Jessica asked Ellen the next morning. She and Elizabeth had caught up with Ellen outside their classroom door.

Ellen shook her head. Jessica walked in first. Caroline and Andy were already in their seats. A few other boys and girls were looking at the class hamsters, Tinkerbell and Thumbelina.

Mr. Pinecone wasn't there. Neither was Mrs. Becker. There wasn't any teacher at all.

"I wonder if he's coming back," Jessica said to Elizabeth.

Elizabeth shrugged. "Maybe Mrs. Becker is better already. Maybe she's coming back today. I sure hope so."

"Maybe we'll get a different substitute," Lila said.

"We sure scared Mr. Pinecone," Charlie said.

Jerry laughed. "Yeah."

"Let's sit in different seats again," Charlie said to everyone. He and Jerry were busy making paper airplanes.

Jessica sat at Ricky Capaldo's regular desk. Lila sat next to her, but Elizabeth didn't sit down right away.

"What's wrong, Lizzie?" Jessica asked. "Sit with us."

"I don't think we should change seats,"

28

Elizabeth answered. She looked over at the door, and her expression changed.

"What is it?" Jessica whispered, turning around.

A very tall man with black hair and a mustache walked into the room. He put some books down on Mrs. Becker's desk with a loud WHAM!

Everyone stopped talking immediately. Anyone who was still standing sat down. Elizabeth was glad she was at her own desk.

"Good morning, class," the new substitute said in a no-nonsense voice. He looked around the room slowly.

When he got to Charlie, he stopped. He didn't say anything for about three seconds. Jessica held her breath.

"Is this science class?" the teacher asked Charlie.

Charlie looked surprised. "No."

"Then you aren't learning how airplanes fly, is that right?" the man went on.

Charlie's face turned pink. He unfolded his paper airplane and stuck the paper in his notebook.

"Fine," the substitute said pleasantly. "My name is Mr. Marshall." He looked around again, and then turned to the blackboard to write his name. Not one single wad of paper flew across the room.

"I know all the tricks," Mr. Marshall continued, underlining his name three times. "If anyone wants to change seats before I take attendance, this would be a good time."

No one said a word. Jessica's cheeks felt hot. She looked at Lila and gulped. Mr. Marshall still stood with his back to the class, waiting.

Everyone who was sitting in the wrong seat stood up and rushed to their own chairs. Jessica flopped into her regular seat next to Elizabeth. In three seconds, the room was completely silent again.

Mr. Marshall finally turned around. He smiled. "Fine. I'm glad we're getting the day off to a good start."

CHAPTER 5

Mysterious Mr. Marshall

Elizabeth was hanging upside down from the jungle gym, pretending to be a monkey. She looked over at her mother, who was sitting on a bench with Mrs. Sutton. They looked upside down to Elizabeth. So did everything else in the park.

"Want to play freeze tag?" Amy asked from below. "Enough kids are here now."

Almost every Saturday, kids from Sweet Valley Elementary came to Charles Freemont Park. Parents took turns coming to watch.

"OK," Elizabeth agreed as she took hold of

the bars and dropped down. She looked around for her sister. Jessica, Lila, and Ellen were on the swings. "Hey, Jessica! Hey, you guys!"

Jessica pumped one more time before she answered. "What?"

"Want to play freeze tag?" Amy yelled.

"Who's It?" Lila wanted to know.

"I call I'm It," Amy said quickly. Amy loved being It, especially since she could run very fast and catch almost anybody.

Lots of other kids came up to the jungle gym. "Hi," Elizabeth said to Todd. He pulled on her ponytail, and then ducked under one of the bars to get away.

Elizabeth giggled and stuck her tongue out at him.

Jessica ran up to them. "Where are the bases?" she asked, panting. In freeze tag,

34

whoever is It can freeze the other players by touching them—except when they're touching the bases.

"I call no bases," Ken Matthews said.

"What?" Winston crossed his eyes. "You're as mean as Mr. Marshall!"

"He's not really mean," Elizabeth said. "He's just strict."

"Strict?" Jessica blurted out. "I think Mr. Marshall's horrible. He yelled at me three times yesterday!"

"Yeah, but you were talking when he said not to," Todd pointed out.

Jessica pretended not to hear him. She bent down to tie her sneakers again.

"I wish Mrs. Becker would come back," Lois said.

Everyone nodded, even though nobody ever wanted to agree with crybaby Lois.

Suddenly, Winston gasped. "Hey! Look!"

They all looked in the direction he was pointing. Elizabeth saw Mr. Marshall walking along the sidewalk.

"I wonder what he's doing here," she said.

But the next moment, they all had something else to wonder about.

A police car was slowing down behind him. It stopped, and the window rolled down. Mr. Marshall leaned over to talk to the officers inside.

Amy was chewing her gum so hard Elizabeth could hear it snap. Elizabeth gulped, not even breathing. Why did the police want to talk to their substitute teacher?

Then Mr. Marshall opened the back door and got into the police car. It pulled away from the curb.

"Wow!" Jessica exclaimed. "Did you see that?"

The huge bubble Amy was blowing popped across her nose.

"Do you think they arrested him?" Ken asked in a whisper.

"Maybe he's a bank robber!" Charlie said, as though he hoped it was true.

Lois opened her mouth in shock.

"Shh!" Jessica said quickly. "Our parents might hear you!"

Elizabeth was startled. She had forgotten about her mother and Mrs. Sutton. She looked quickly over her shoulder. They were still sitting on the bench, talking. They didn't seem to notice anything was wrong.

"Why don't you want them to hear?" Todd asked. The others looked puzzled, too.

"They would just get upset," Jessica explained. "If my mom finds out our teacher is a criminal, she'll be really angry!"

Elizabeth realized her sister was right. All their parents would be angry and upset. But what if Mr. Marshall was really being arrested for having done something terrible?

Part of Elizabeth wanted to tell her mother. But part of her agreed with Jessica. Mrs. Wakefield would only start to worry if she knew about Mr. Marshall. Elizabeth didn't want that to happen.

"What should we do?" Amy asked.

"We could follow the police car," Jessica suggested. Charlie nodded eagerly.

"It's already gone," Ken said.

Elizabeth bit her lower lip. "Maybe we should just wait until Monday."

They all looked at each other and nodded. The truth about Mr. Marshall would soon come out.

CHAPTER 6

Best Behavior

Jessica held Elizabeth's hand tightly as they walked to class on Monday. "Do you think he'll be there?" she asked her sister. They had wondered about Mr. Marshall all weekend.

"I don't know," Elizabeth said shaking her head. "Do you?"

"I don't know," Jessica echoed. "Are you scared?"

"No." Elizabeth's blue-green eyes were wide. "Are you?"

Jessica thought about it. She wasn't scared, but she was excited. She wanted to know if Mr. Marshall had been arrested, and if he had, what for! They had never had such an exciting substitute.

When they got to their classroom door, they stopped and looked in. "He's here!" Elizabeth said in surprise.

Almost everyone was already seated. No one was talking, not even Lila or Charlie. Mr. Marshall was at Mrs. Becker's desk, correcting papers. There were five apples on the desk.

"Coming in, girls?" Mr. Marshall's voice made Jessica and Elizabeth both jump. He wasn't even looking at them.

Everyone turned to watch them come inside. Jessica couldn't wait to talk to Lila. She wondered who had brought the apples. A lot of kids seemed to want to be on Mr. Marshall's good side!

When she sat down, somebody tapped her shoulder.

"What?" Jessica whispered, turning around. Todd Wilkins sat behind her. He was holding up a tiny scrap of paper with very small printing on it.

"Maybe he escaped from jail," it read.

Jessica looked at Todd and nodded, grinning. It was like an adventure! Then she looked at Elizabeth. "Psst," she hissed.

Elizabeth glanced over. Todd held the paper so she could read it too. Elizabeth's eyes widened.

"What should we do?" Jessica asked very softly.

"Just don't say anything to get in trouble," Elizabeth warned. "Maybe Mrs. Becker will come back tomorrow."

Jessica nodded. She was so excited, she

couldn't stop smiling. Opening her notebook, she wrote on a piece of paper, "Pass it around. Do what Mr. Marshall says or else he might do something bad." She folded the note and dropped it over her shoulder onto Todd's desk.

Jessica kept a close watch on Mr. Marshall, who was still correcting papers. Everyone in the class was as quiet as mice. Even the kids who weren't at the park on Saturday knew what the rest of them had seen.

Quickly, Jessica took a peek over her shoulder to see who had her note. It was on Lois Waller's desk. Lois was blinking fast, as though she had tears in her eyes.

"Jessica!" Mr. Marshall said suddenly.

Jessica jumped in her seat and swallowed hard. The substitute was looking at her very sharply. He always seemed to know when she was passing notes. Jessica glanced quickly at her sister and cleared her throat. "Yes, sir?" she said in her most polite voice. She was trying to think of a good excuse.

Mr. Marshall stood up from his desk and walked slowly to the front of the class. Jessica wished Lois would be brave enough to eat the note.

"Jessica, I'd like you to—"

Jessica squeezed her eyes shut and crossed her fingers.

"I'd like you to pass out art supplies, please," Mr. Marshall said. "We're going to make get-well cards for Mrs. Becker this morning."

There was a loud hissing noise in the room as everyone let their breath out at the same time. Jessica slumped in her chair. That was a close call! "OK," she squeaked.

Mr. Marshall smiled and sat down again. This time, nothing bad happened. But what would he do next?

CHAPTER 7

Jessica's Great Idea

Elizabeth felt tired when she and Jessica got off at their bus stop. All day long, their whole second-grade class had been very nervous. Everyone was curious about Mr. Marshall.

Elizabeth wasn't really sure he was a crook, though. If he was, why didn't Mrs. Armstrong, the principal, know? And why wouldn't he be in jail? It didn't make any sense. The more she thought about it, the dumber it seemed.

"Hey, you guys!" the twins' older brother, Steven, shouted to them. Steven was in fifth grade, and usually he acted as though he didn't know who they were. But today, he was running to catch up with them.

"What?" Jessica asked as she tried to balance her books on her head.

"I heard about your sub," Steven said, walking next to his twin sisters. "Did he really escape from prison?"

Elizabeth started to say "No," but Jessica interrupted.

"I think so," Jessica agreed. "That's what everybody thinks. He's got this mean way of staring at you."

"Wow." Steven looked impressed. "I wish we had him. You know what I would do?" he asked in a boastful voice.

Elizabeth arched her eyebrows. "What?"

"I'd *make* him tell us what he did," Steven bragged. "I would."

48

Elizabeth knew her brother was just showing off. If Mr. Marshall was really a crook, no fifth grader would scare him! Besides, maybe he wasn't a crook at all. Then he would just think Steven was nuts.

"Hey!" Jessica gasped. She stopped on the sidewalk and turned to them both. "You know what we should really do? Set some kind of a trap for him. We could catch him, and take him to the police!"

"Yeah!" Steven agreed eagerly. "Good idea!"

Elizabeth wrinkled her nose. "You guys . . ." she said.

Jessica and Steven didn't hear her. They were busy arguing about how to set a trap for Mr. Marshall. Elizabeth raised her voice. "You GUYS!"

They both stopped talking. "What?" Jessica said. "Do you have an idea?"

"I just think there's probably a reason why Mr. Marshall went with those policemen."

"Liz!" Jessica exclaimed. "We all saw Mr. Marshall being arrested."

"Then how come he's still our substitute teacher?" Elizabeth asked.

"Because he escaped."

"I know," Steven cut in. "He's hiding out. Nobody would ever look for him in the elementary school, right? It's the perfect disguise!"

"Right!" Jessica agreed happily. She gave Elizabeth an I-told-you-so look. "He's hiding out," she repeated. "And I still say we should try to capture him."

Elizabeth shrugged and switched her books to her other arm. "OK, Jessica. If you really think he's a crook, and you really think you can capture him, go ahead." She

51

started walking toward their house. She was getting hungry for a snack.

"Wait, Liz!" Jessica yelled. "You have to help!"

Elizabeth turned and walked backward so she could see her sister and brother and still walk home. She shook her head. "It's the dumbest thing I ever heard of!" she called. "I don't think he's an escaped crook."

"You'll see!" Jessica pouted.

Elizabeth shrugged. She was sure there would be a simple explanation for why Mr. Marshall had gone with the police. But what that explanation could be, she had no idea!

CHAPTER 8

Tattoos

During recess, Jessica, Elizabeth, and Amy all crowded around Lila.

"First you need the right kind of pen," Lila explained. She was showing them how to make tattoos.

"All criminals have tattoos on their arms," Lila said in a know-it-all way.

"You're right," Jessica agreed. "I wonder if Mr. Marshall has one."

Lila opened her shiny gold-colored purse and took out a green pen and a piece of paper. She smoothed the paper out on her leg. "What kind of design do you want?" she asked Jessica. "Heart? Flower?"

"Ummm . . ." Jessica bit her bottom lip and looked at her sister. "What kind are you going to have, Lizzie?"

Elizabeth shrugged. "I don't know. How about flowers?"

"Can I have my name?" Amy asked.

Lila nodded. "But you have to write it backwards. Watch."

With her pen, she carefully drew a flower with five petals. Then she pressed hard on the lines over and over again with the pen.

"OK, where do you want it?" she asked Jessica.

Jessica frowned. "On my arm." She pushed up her sleeve.

"You have to lick the spot, first," Lila said.

After Jessica stretched her arm so she could lick her skin, Lila pressed the flower picture on the wet spot. She rubbed the paper

hard, and then peeled it off. The ink from the paper was now on Jessica's arm.

"Hey!" Amy said. "Neat! Do mine!"

Lila had a show-off smile on her face. "You try it. I'll watch."

Elizabeth and Amy took turns making tattoos. Amy wrote her name backwards. When she pressed it on the back of her hand, the writing came out the correct way.

"I'm doing another one," Jessica decided. "This time I want a—"

She broke off in the middle of her sentence and stared out at the parking lot.

"Look, you guys!" she exclaimed. "A police car!"

The others looked, too. Almost everyone on the playground had stopped what they were doing and were also looking. Jessica could hear kids starting to whisper. A police officer got out and walked toward the school building.

"Do you think he's coming to arrest Mr. Marshall again?" Amy asked breathlessly.

Elizabeth's mouth was open. "I don't know!"

"Let's go see!" Jessica said, jumping up. "There might be a showdown!"

Ken, Todd, and Winston were standing near them. "Are you going to see what's happening?" Todd asked the girls.

Jessica nodded. "Come on!"

They all started running for Mrs. Becker's room. Other kids followed behind. Up ahead, they saw the policeman open the classroom door.

"Come on!" everyone yelled. "Let's go!"

CHAPTER 9

The Confession

All the kids in Mrs. Becker's class tried to crowd through the doorway at once. Elizabeth, Jessica, Lila, and Todd were in front. They stumbled inside, and then stopped.

Mr. Marshall and the policeman were facing each other, but they turned as the twins, Lila, and Todd popped into the room.

No one said a word. Elizabeth could hear her heart pounding. *What was going on?*

"Come on in, everyone!" Mr. Marshall said. "Take your seats."

Completely silent, everyone in Mrs.

Becker's class came in and sat down. Jessica took hold of Elizabeth's hand and squeezed it. All eyes were on Mr. Marshall and the policeman. A bunch of kids from other classes stood outside the door to spy on them.

When everyone was seated, Mr. Marshall folded his arms across his chest. His dark eyebrows looked very fierce. "This will be my last day here," he began.

"See! See!" Jessica whispered excitedly. "They're taking him away!" Elizabeth put her finger to her lips and shook her head.

"I want you all to meet somebody," Mr. Marshall went on. "This is Sergeant Polk, my partner on the police force."

Elizabeth stared at them. She was confused. *Partner?*

Everyone else looked confused, too. Mr. Marshall raised his eyebrows. He looked like he was going to laugh.

"I'm a police officer, too," Mr. Marshall went on. "Right now I'm on the night shift, and that's why I can be a substitute during school hours."

Elizabeth felt her cheeks turn pink. Mr. Marshall wasn't a crook! He was a policeman! She looked over at her sister. Jessica also looked embarrassed.

Mr. Marshall wasn't gruff and firm because he was a dangerous criminal. He was that way because he was just the opposite! In fact, he was actually a little bit like Mrs. Becker. She was very firm, but very fair, too.

"That's right," Sergeant Polk said. He smiled. "Mr. Marshall heard the stories that have been going around school, and he decided to set the record straight."

Somebody in the back of the classroom giggled. It sounded like Charlie Cashman, but Elizabeth didn't turn around to look. In-

stead, she felt like giggling, too. Everything seemed funny, now.

"Psst!" Elizabeth heard. She glanced at her sister. "I knew it," Jessica whispered. "I knew it all the time."

Elizabeth rolled her eyes. "You did not!"

One by one, the kids started raising their hands to ask questions. Elizabeth smiled to herself. She had guessed there was a simple explanation, but she had never guessed what it was!

"I hope we get him next time Mrs. Becker gets sick, don't you?" she asked her sister.

"I sure do!"

"But you'd better not talk in class anymore," Elizabeth warned. "Or else he might put you in jail."

Jessica stuck her tongue out at Elizabeth, but she was smiling.

"OK, class," Mr. Marshall said. "I think it's time to get to work now. And, please," he added, "stop staring at me like I'm going to hold up a bank, OK?"

"OK," everyone said at the same time.

"Fine," Mr. Marshall said. "Now let's start putting math homework problems up on the board. I want Mrs. Becker to be satisfied when she comes back tomorrow."

Elizabeth blinked in surprise. "She's coming back tomorrow?" she blurted out.

"That's right," Mr. Marshall said. "*Everything* will be back to normal."

CHAPTER 10

Mrs. Becker Returns

"Good morning, girls!" Mrs. Becker said as Jessica and Elizabeth burst into their classroom.

"Hi!" Jessica and Elizabeth said at the same time.

"Are you feeling better?" Elizabeth added.

Mrs. Becker smiled. "Much better, thank you. I'm glad to be back."

Everyone else looked very happy, too. Things were definitely back to normal. Lila was showing Ellen and Caroline a new eraser in the shape of a banana, but she wasn't letting them try it. Charlie was boasting to some of the other boys about his bi-cycle. Sandy and Amy were feeding the hamsters, and Andy was trying to make his messy notebook look neater. Lois was scratching some dried egg off her shirt.

Jessica sat down in her chair. "Boy, this is a lot better," she sighed. Elizabeth nodded.

"I have an announcement, class!" Mrs. Becker called.

The kids who weren't sitting down quickly went to their seats. Mrs. Becker stood up, smiling.

"First of all, thank you for behaving so well for the substitute," she began.

Jessica looked over at her twin. They both grinned.

"And second of all," the teacher continued. "Has anyone ever heard of Jamaica?"

The room was silent. Then Lila raised her hand. "Yes, Lila?" Mrs. Becker asked.

Lila folded her hands. "Jamaica is a tropical island. I went there once for vacation," she said with her nose in the air.

"That's right." Mrs. Becker pointed to the United States map. "Do you see this part of the ocean, here, south of Florida? These are the islands of the West Indies."

Jessica squinched her eyes. All she could see from her seat were a bunch of little spots on the blue background. She looked over at Lila and pouted. Lila had been on airplanes six different times, and often acted as though she knew everything.

Mrs. Becker sat at her desk again. "Jamaica is one of those islands. We're going to have a new student from Jamaica be part of our class, starting next week."

"Is it a boy or a girl?" Winston called out without raising his hand.

"A girl," Mrs. Becker answered.

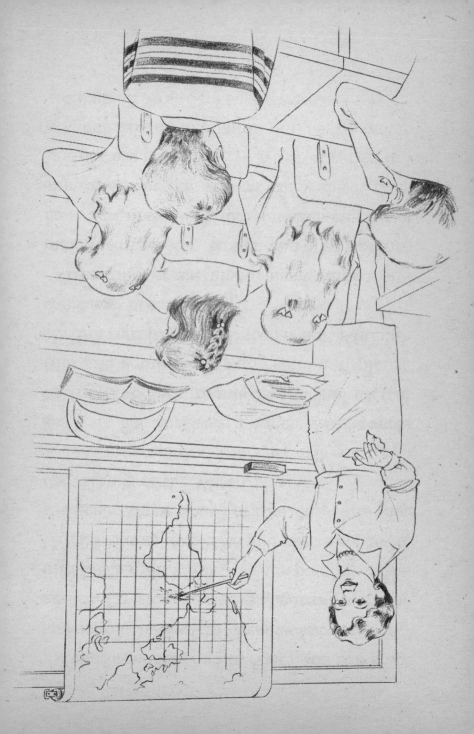

"Yea," said the girls. "Boo," said the boys.

Jessica was excited there would be a new girl in the class. She hoped the girl would be fun to play with.

"Her name is Eva," the teacher explained. "And I'm going to pick someone to be her special welcome host. That person will show Eva around and help her feel at home."

"Mrs. Becker?" Lila asked raising her hand. "Since I've been to Jamaica, could I be the welcome host?"

Mrs. Becker pursed her lips. "Well . . . we'll see, Lila."

Jessica frowned. Lila always wanted to get picked for special things. But just because Lila had been to Jamaica didn't mean she should be chosen. Jessica knew she'd make the perfect host.

This time, Jessica wanted to be the one to get picked.

Who will get to be Eva's welcome host? And what will the new girl be like? Find out in Sweet Valley Kids #4, ELIZABETH'S VALENTINE.

Great new series!
Be a part of

SWEET VALLEY KIDS

Jessica and Elizabeth have had lots of adventures in *Sweet Valley High* and *Sweet Valley Twins*...now read about the twins at age seven! You'll love all the fun that comes with being seven—birthday parties, playing dress-up, class projects, putting on puppet shows and plays, losing a tooth, setting up lemonade stands, caring for animals and much more! It's all part of SWEET VALLEY KIDS. Read them all!

☐ **SURPRISE! SURPRISE! #1**
15782-2 $2.75/$3.25

☐ **RUNAWAY HAMSTER #2**
15759-0 $2.75/$3.25

☐ **THE TWINS' MYSTERY TEACHER # 3**
15760-4 $2.75/$3.25

- -

SWEET VALLEY TWINS

Buy them at your local bookstore or use this handy page for ordering:

Bantam Books, Dept. SVT3, 414 East Golf Road, Des Plaines, IL 60016

Please send me the items I have checked above. I am enclosing $_____
(please add $2.00 to cover postage and handling). Send check or money
order, no cash or C.O.D.s please.

Mr/Ms _____

Address _____

City/State _____ Zip _____

Please allow four to six weeks for delivery.   SVT3-9/89
Prices and availability subject to change without notice.